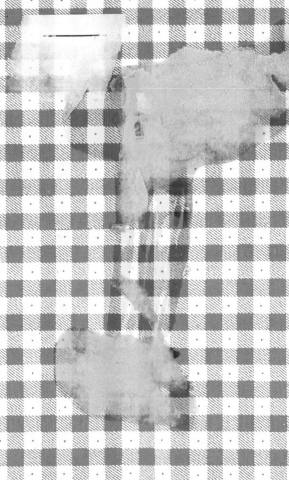

MY FIRST LITTLE HOUSE BOOKS

GOING WEST

ADAPTED FROM THE LITTLE HOUSE BOOKS

By Laura Ingalls Wilder

Illustrated by Renée Graef

HARPERCOLLINS PUBLISHERS

For my mother, Grace
—R.G.

Going West   Text adapted from Little House on the Prairie, copyright 1935 by Laura Ingalls Wilder, renewed 1963 by Roger Lea MacBride.
Illustrations © 1996 by Renée Graef. Illustrations were prepared with the help of Doris Ettlinger and Cathy Holly. Printed in the U.S.A.
All rights reserved. Wilder, Laura Ingalls, 1867–1957.   Going west / adapted from the little house books by Laura Ingalls Wilder ;
illustrated by Renée Graef.   p.   cm. — (My first little house books)   Summary: A young pioneer girl and her family prepare to leave
the big woods of Wisconsin and travel west in their covered wagon. ISBN 0-06-027167-1. — ISBN 0-06-027168-X (lib. bdg.)
[1. Frontier and pioneer life—Fiction.]   I. Graef, Renée, ill.   II. Title.   III. Series.
PZ7.W6461Gr 1996 [E]—dc20 95-35721 CIP AC
1 2 3 4 5 6 7 8 9 10 ❖ First Edition
HarperCollins®, 🏠®, and Little House® are trademarks of HarperCollins Publishers Inc.

Illustrations for the My First Little House Books are
inspired by the work of Garth Williams with his
permission, which we gratefully acknowledge.

Once upon a time, a little girl named Laura
lived in the Big Woods of Wisconsin in a little house
made of logs. Laura lived in the little house with her
Pa, her Ma, her big sister Mary, her baby sister
Carrie, and their good old bulldog Jack.

Many people had come to live in the Big Woods. Almost every day Laura and Mary stopped their playing to look in surprise at a wagon slowly creaking by.

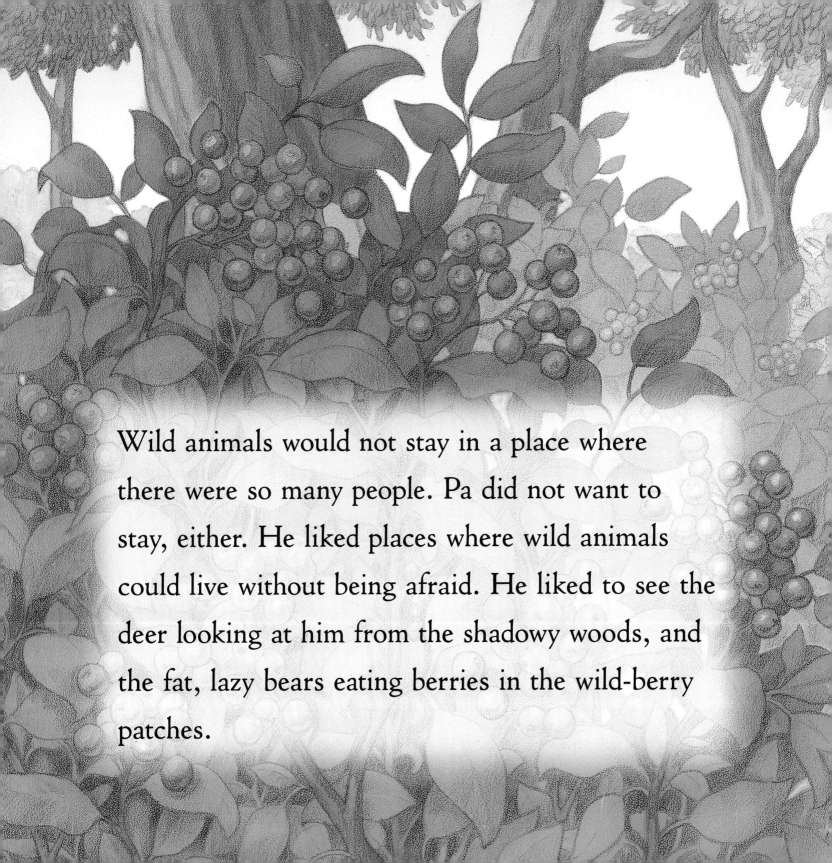

Wild animals would not stay in a place where
there were so many people. Pa did not want to
stay, either. He liked places where wild animals
could live without being afraid. He liked to see the
deer looking at him from the shadowy woods, and
the fat, lazy bears eating berries in the wild-berry
patches.

One long winter evening Pa told Ma that he was going to take the family to live in the West.

In the West there were not as many people, there were no trees, and the grass grew thick and high.

So Pa sold the little house in the Big Woods.
He sold the cow and calf, too.

Pa made hickory bows and fastened them to the wagon. Ma helped him stretch white canvas over the bows to make a covered wagon for the family to travel in. Then they packed up everything in the little house, except for the beds and tables and chairs. They did not need to take these, because Pa could always make new ones.

Then one morning before it was even light outside, Ma gently shook Mary and Laura until they woke up.

Laura and Mary put on their long red-flannel underwear, their wool petticoats and wool dresses, and their long wool stockings. Next they put on their coats, their rabbit-skin hoods, and their red yarn mittens.

Outside the little house there was snow on the ground, and the air was still and cold and dark. Through the gray woods came lanterns with wagons and horses, bringing Grandma and Grandpa and aunts and uncles and cousins.

Mary and Laura held on tightly to their dolls
and did not say a word. Grandma and the aunts

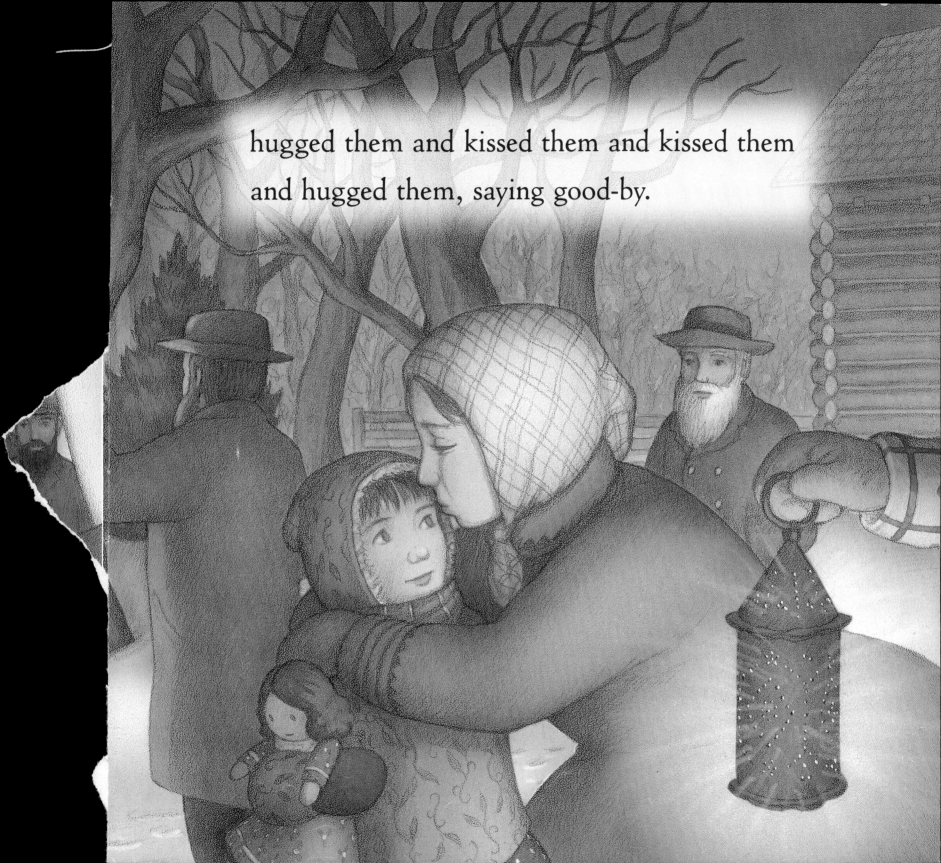

hugged them and kissed them and kissed them
and hugged them, saying good-by.

The uncles helped Pa hitch the horses to the
wagon. All the cousins were told to kiss Laura
and Mary, and so they did.

Then Pa picked up Mary and Laura and set them in the wagon. He helped Ma climb up onto the wagon seat, and Grandma reached up and gave her baby Carrie.

Off went the wagon, and the little house in the
Big Woods stayed inside the log fence, behind the

big trees that Mary and Laura liked to play under.
And that was the last they saw of the little house.

The family had a long journey ahead of them.
But Pa was on the wagon seat and Jack was under
the wagon, and Laura felt happy knowing they
were on their way to another little house, a little
house on the Western prairie.

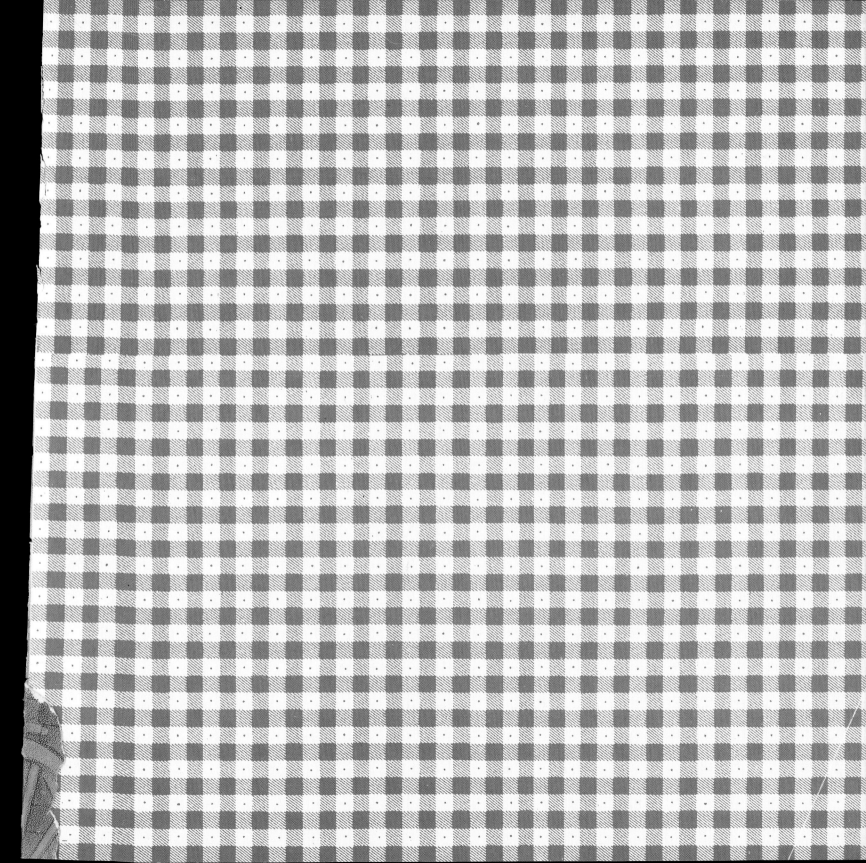